For James the Cake
and for Mack ... our dog.

Our Bloomsbury Book House
has a special room for each
age group –
this one is from the Nursery.

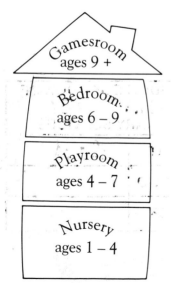

Gamesroom
ages 9 +

Bedroom
ages 6 – 9

Playroom
ages 4 – 7

Nursery
ages 1 – 4

First Published in Great Britain in 1995
Bloomsbury Publishing Plc, 38 Soho Square, London W1V 5DF
This edition published 1997

Copyright © Text and illustrations Bernice Lum 1995
The moral right of the author has been asserted
A CIP catalogue record of this book is available from the
British Library

ISBN 0 7475 3066 1

Manufactured in China

10 9 8 7 6 5 4 3 2 1

If I Had a Dog

Bernice Lum

Bloomsbury Children's Books

If I had a dog ...

I would call him Stanley

I would teach him to talk ...

and to read.

I would teach him to sing ...

and to dance.

and to skip ...

and to make a cup of tea, hee hee.

and to balance things.

I would teach him to roller-skate ...

and even to ride a bicycle.

Most of all ...

I would teach him that I am his friend.